When I Was King

by Linda Ashman

illustrated by David McPhail

HarperCollins Publishers

Before you came, I owned the throne.

They trembled at my slightest moan.

I was the star,

the prize,

the king. . . .

But **you** have ruined

everything.

I'm the one who hops and skips,
sings and dances, spins and flips.
But no one sees a thing I do—
they never take their eyes off

YOU!

You **yawn**, they **laugh**.

You **snort**, they **cheer**.

You **drool**, they **smile**

from **ear** to **ear.**

You **burp**, they **giggle**

with **delight. . . .**

But if **I** do, it's not polite.

Before you came, this tub was mine.
This soap was mine. This sub was mine.

This train was **mine**.
This hat was **mine**.

This boat was **mine**.

This bat was **mine**.

This drum. This book.

This bear was **mine**.

This ball.

This brush.

This chair was **mine**.

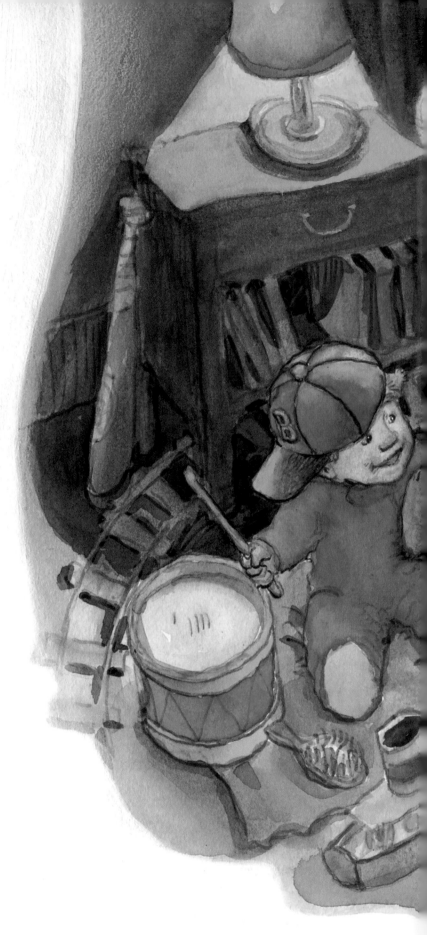

This chalk.

This truck.

This blanket, too.

The whole wide world was **mine**—till you.

Today you dribbled on my clothes,

yanked my hair,

pulled my nose,

ripped my book,

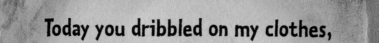

threw my dragon,

tipped my tower,

broke my wagon.

But when you gnawed
my catcher's mitt,
I got so mad, I threw a fit.
I flung my body on the floor

and screamed

until my throat was sore.

I looked at Mama. Thought she'd shout.
Thought I'd get a long time-out.
Instead, she held me very tight.
And whispered softly,
"It's all right."

She told me, "Baby's very small.
Really can't do much at all.
But **look at you!**
Look how you've grown!
There's so much you can do alone!"

This afternoon,
I cleaned my shelf,

made a sandwich by myself,

brushed the dogs,

fed the fishes,

pushed the vacuum,

washed my dishes.

Filled your bottle,

fetched the mail,

dumped your stinky

diaper pail,

raked the leaves into a heap

(all **you** did was eat and sleep!).

Mama hugged me.
Papa smiled.
Grandma said,
"You darling child!"

Grandpa made my favorite treat.
(**You** got mashed-up peas to eat.)

Tonight I helped you in the bath.
I washed your toes. I made you laugh.
And when I came to say goodnight,
I **liked** the way you squeezed me tight.

Before you came,
when I was king,
I didn't want to change a thing.
I liked to rule the world alone. . . .

But maybe
I can share my throne.